Stories from

Winnie
-the-
Pooh

"I wish to pay tribute to the work of E. H. Shepard
which has been inspirational in the creation
of these new drawings." *Andrew Grey*

EGMONT

We bring stories to life

This edition first published in Great Britain in 2006 by Dean,
an imprint of Egmont UK Limited
239 Kensington High Street, London W8 6SA.
Illustrated by Andrew Grey.
Based on the 'Winnie-the-Pooh' works
By A. A. Milne and E. H. Shepard.
Text ©The Trustees of the Pooh Properties.
Illustrations © 2003, 2005 Disney Enterprises, Inc.

ISBN 978 0 6035 6238 9
ISBN 0 6035 6238 8
1 3 5 7 9 10 8 6 4 2
Printed in China

Stories from

Winnie
-the-
Pooh

DEAN

Contents

Pooh Goes Visiting

Winnie-the-Pooh was walking through the Forest, humming proudly to himself. He had made up a little hum as he was doing his **Stoutness Exercises** in front of the glass:

Tra-la-la, tra-la-la,

as he stretched up as high as he could go, and then

Tra-la-la, tra-la-la oh help! la,

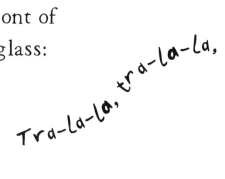

as he tried to reach his toes.

After breakfast he had learnt it off by heart, and now he was humming it right through, properly. It went like this:

Tra-la-la tra-la-la
Tra-la-la, tra-la-la,
Rum-tum-
tiddle-um-tum.
Tiddle-iddle tiddle-iddle,
Tiddle-iddle, tiddle-iddle,
Rum-tum-tum-tiddle-um.

Pooh was humming this hum to himself, when
suddenly he came to a sandy bank, and in the bank
was a large hole.

"Aha!" said Pooh. (*Rum-tum-tiddle-um-tum.*) "If I know
anything about anything, that hole means Rabbit and
Rabbit means Company, and Company means Food
and such like. *Rum-tum-tum-tiddle-um.*"

So he bent down, put his head into the hole, and called
out: "Is anybody at home?"

There was a sudden scuffling noise from inside the hole,
and then silence.

"What I said was, 'Is anybody at home?'" called out Pooh
very loudly.

"No!" said a voice; and then added, "You needn't shout,
I heard you quite well the first time."

"Bother!" said Pooh. "Isn't there anybody here at all?"

"Nobody."

Pooh thought to himself, "There must be somebody there, because **somebody** must have said 'Nobody.'" So he put his head back in the hole, and said: "Well, could you very kindly tell me where Rabbit is?"

12

"He has gone to see his friend Pooh Bear," said Rabbit.

"But this is Me!" said Pooh, very much surprised.

"Are you sure?" said Rabbit, still more surprised.

"Quite, quite sure," said Pooh.

"Oh, well then, come in."

So Pooh pushed
and pushed and pushed
his way through the hole, and at last he got in.
"You were quite right," said Rabbit, looking at him
all over. "It is you. Glad to see you."
"Who did you think it was?"
"Well, I wasn't sure. You know how it is in the Forest.
One can't have anybody coming into one's house. One
has to be careful. What about a mouthful of *something*?"

Pooh **always** liked a little *something* at eleven o'clock in the morning, and he was very glad to see Rabbit getting out the plates and mugs. When Rabbit said, "**Honey** or **condensed milk** with your bread?" he was so excited that he said, "**Both**," and then, so as not to seem greedy, he added, "But don't bother about the bread, please." And for a **long time** after that he said nothing.

At last, humming to himself in a rather sticky voice, Pooh got up, shook Rabbit lovingly by the paw, and said that he must be going on.

"Must you?" said Rabbit politely.

"Well," said Pooh, "I could stay a little longer if it – if you –" and he tried very hard to look in the direction of the larder.

"As a matter of fact," said Rabbit, "I was going out myself directly."

"Oh well, then, I'll be going on. Goodbye."

"Well, goodbye, if you're sure you won't have any more."

"Is there any more?" asked Pooh quickly.

Rabbit took the covers off the dishes and said, "No, there wasn't."

"I thought not," said Pooh, nodding to himself.

"Well, goodbye. I must be going on."

So he started to climb out of the hole.

He pulled
with his
front paws,
and pushed
with his
back paws,
and in a
little while
his nose was out
in the open again . . .

and then his ears . . . and then his front paws . . .
and then his shoulders . . .
and then –

"Oh, help!" said Pooh.
"I'd better go back."
"Oh, bother!" said Pooh.
"I shall have to go on."
"I can't do either!" said Pooh...
"Oh, help and bother!"

Now, by this time Rabbit wanted
to go for a walk too, and finding the
front door **full**, he went out by
the back door, and came
round to Pooh, and
looked at him.

"Hallo, are you stuck?" he asked.

"N-no," said Pooh carelessly. "Just resting and thinking and humming to myself."

"Here, give us a paw," said Rabbit.

Pooh Bear stretched out a paw, and Rabbit pulled and pulled and pulled . . .

"Ow!" cried Pooh. "You're hurting!"

"The fact is," said Rabbit, "you're stuck."

"It all comes," said Pooh crossly, "of not having front doors big enough."

"It all comes," said Rabbit sternly, "of eating too much. Well, well, I shall go and fetch Christopher Robin."

Christopher Robin lived at the other end of the Forest. When he came back with Rabbit, and saw the front half of Pooh sticking out of the hole, he said, "Silly old Bear," in such a loving voice that everybody felt quite hopeful again.

"I was just beginning to think," said Pooh, sniffing slightly, "that Rabbit might never be able to use his front door again. And I should hate that," he said.

"So should I," said Rabbit.

"Of course he'll use his front door again," said Christopher Robin.

"Good," said Rabbit.

"If we can't pull you out, Pooh, we might push you back."

Rabbit scratched his whiskers thoughtfully, and pointed out that when Pooh was pushed back, he was back where he started –

"You mean I'd never get out?" said Pooh.

"I mean," said Rabbit, "that having got so far, it seems a pity to waste it."

Christopher Robin nodded.

"Then there's only one thing to be done," he said. "We shall have to wait for you to get thin again."

"How long does getting thin take?" asked Pooh anxiously.

"About a week, I should think," said Christopher Robin.

"But I can't stay here for a week!"

"You can stay here all right, silly old Bear. It's getting you out which is so difficult."

"We'll read to you," said Rabbit cheerfully. "And I say, you're taking up a good deal of room in my house – do you mind if I use your back legs as a **towel-rail**? Because, I mean, there they are – doing nothing – and it would be very convenient just to hang the towels on them."

"**A week!**" said Pooh gloomily. "What about meals?"

"I'm afraid no meals," said Christopher Robin, "because of getting thin **quicker**. But we will read to you."

Pooh began to sigh, and then found he couldn't because he was so **tightly stuck**; and a tear rolled down his eye as he said: "Then would you read a **Sustaining Book**, such as would help and comfort a **Wedged Bear in Great Tightness?**"

So for a week Christopher Robin read that sort of book at the **North end** of Pooh,

and Rabbit hung his washing on the South end . . .
and in between, Pooh felt himself getting slenderer
and slenderer.

Then at the end of the week
Christopher Robin took hold of
Pooh's front paws while Rabbit
took hold of Christopher Robin, and
all Rabbit's friends and relations
took hold of Rabbit, and then
Christopher Robin said, "Now!"and
they **all pulled together** . . .
And for a long time Pooh
only said "Ow!"
And "Oh!"

And then, all of a sudden, he went:

"Pop!"

just as if a cork
were coming out of a bottle.
And Christopher Robin and Rabbit and all
Rabbit's friends and relations went **head-over-heels**
backwards . . . and on the top of them came
Winnie-the-Pooh – free at last.

So, with a nod of thanks to his friends, he went on with his walk through the forest, humming proudly to himself. Christopher Robin looked after him lovingly, and said to himself, "Silly old Bear!"

Piglet Meets
a Heffalump

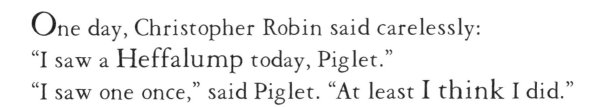

One day, Christopher Robin said carelessly:
"I saw a Heffalump today, Piglet."
"I saw one once," said Piglet. "At least I think I did."

"So did I," said Pooh, wondering what a Heffalump
was like.

Then they talked about something else, until it was
time for Pooh and Piglet to go home.

As they came to the Six Pine Trees, Pooh said:
"Piglet, I have decided to catch a Heffalump."
Pooh waited for Piglet to say "How?" but Piglet
said nothing. The fact was, Piglet was wishing
that *he* had thought of it first.

"I shall do it," said Pooh, "by means of a Trap.
It must be a Cunning Trap, so you will have
to help me, Piglet."
"How shall we do it?" said Piglet.
And they sat down to think it out.

Pooh's idea was that they should dig a Very Deep
Pit, and the Heffalump would come and fall in.
"Why would he fall in?" said Piglet.
Pooh said the Heffalump might be looking up at
the sky, wondering if it would rain, so he wouldn't
see the Very Deep Pit until he was half-way
down it.

Pooh felt sure that a bear with a Very Clever Brain could catch a Heffalump if he knew the **right way**. "Suppose," he said to Piglet, "*you* wanted to catch *me*, how would you do it?"

"Well," said Piglet. "I should make a Trap, put a Jar of Honey in and you would smell it and go in after it, and –" "And I should lick round the edges first and then the middle and then –" said Pooh excitedly.

"Yes, well never mind about that," said Piglet. "The first thing to think of is, What do Heffalumps like? I should think haycorns, shouldn't you?"

Pooh, who had gone into a happy dream, woke with a start, and said Honey was a much more trappy thing than Haycorns.

"All right, *I'll* dig the pit, while *you* go and get the honey," said Piglet.

"Very well," said Pooh and he stumped off.

As soon as he got home, he took down a large jar from the top shelf. It had HUNNY written on it. He took a large lick. "Yes," he said, "it is. No doubt about that!" and he gave a deep sigh. Having made certain, he took the jar back to Piglet.

Piglet said, "Is that all you've got left?" and Pooh said, "Yes." Because it was. So Piglet put the jar at the bottom of the Pit and they went off home together. "Good night," said Piglet. "And we meet at six o'clock tomorrow morning and see how many Heffalumps we've got in our Trap."

Some hours later, Pooh woke up. He was hungry. He went to the larder, stood on a chair and reached to the top shelf and found – nothing.
"That's funny," he thought. "I know I had a jar of honey there. Then he began murmuring a murmur to himself:

It's very, very funny,
'cos I know I had some honey;
'Cos it had a label on,
saying HUNNY.

A goloptious full-up pot too,
And I don't know where it's got to,
No, I don't know where it's gone —
Well, it's funny.

Suddenly he remembered. He had put it into the Cunning Trap. He got back into bed but he couldn't sleep. He tried counting Heffalumps but every Heffalump was making straight for Pooh's honey, *and eating it all*. Pooh could bear it no longer. He jumped out of bed and ran to the Six Pine Trees.

In the half-light the Very Deep Pit seemed deeper. Pooh climbed in. "Bother!" said Pooh, as he got his nose inside the jar. "A Heffalump has been eating it!"

And then he thought a little and said, "Oh, no *I* did. I forgot." But there was a little left at the **very bottom** and he **pushed** his head right in, and began to **lick** . . .

By and by Piglet woke up. He didn't feel very brave. What was a Heffalump like? Was it Fierce? Wouldn't it be better to pretend he had a headache, and couldn't go to the Six Pine Trees? But suppose it was a very fine day, and there was no Heffalump in the Trap, here he would be, simply wasting his time for nothing. What should he do?

48

Then he had a Clever Idea. He would go now, peep into the Trap and see if there was a Heffalump there. If there was, he would go back to bed, and if there wasn't, he wouldn't. So off he went.

As he got nearer he could hear it heffalumping about like anything.

"Oh, dear, oh, dear, oh, dear!" said Piglet to himself. He wanted to run away but felt he must just see what a Heffalump was like. So he crept to the side of the Trap and looked in . . .

And all the time Winnie-the-Pooh had been trying to get the honey-jar off his head. He tried bumping it against things and tried to climb out of the Trap, but couldn't find his way. At last he lifted his head, jar and all, and made a roaring noise of Sadness and Despair . . . and it was at that moment that Piglet looked down.

"Help, help!" cried Piglet. "Horrible Heffalump!" and he scampered off as hard as he could. He didn't stop crying and scampering until he got to Christopher Robin's house.

"Whatever's the matter?" said Christopher Robin.
"Heff," said Piglet, "a Heff – a Heff – a Heffalump."
"What did it look like?"
"It had the biggest head you ever saw. A huge big – I don't know – like an enormous nothing. Like a jar."
"Well," said Christopher Robin, "I shall go and look at it. Come on."

"I can hear it, can't you?" said Piglet anxiously,
as they got near.
"I can hear something," said Christopher Robin.
It was Pooh bumping his head against a tree-root.
"There!" said Piglet. And he held on tight to
Christopher Robin's hand.

Suddenly Christopher Robin began to laugh . . .
And while he was still laughing – Crash went the
Heffalump's head against the tree-root, Smash
went the jar, and out came Pooh's head again . . .

Then Piglet saw what a Foolish Piglet he had
been, and he was so ashamed that he ran straight
home and went to bed. Christopher Robin and Pooh
went home to breakfast together.

"Oh, Bear!" said Christopher Robin.
"How I do love you!"
"So do I," said Pooh.

Eeyore Has a Birthday

Eeyore stood by the stream, and looked at himself in the water.

"Pathetic," he said. "That's what it is. Pathetic." He turned, splashed across the stream and turned to look at himself in the water again. "As I thought," he said. "No better from this side. But nobody cares." There was a crackling noise in the bracken, and out came Pooh.

"Good morning, Eeyore," said Pooh.

"Good morning, Pooh Bear," said Eeyore, gloomily. "If it is a good morning, which I doubt."

"Oh!" said Pooh and he sat down on a large stone and sang Cottleston Pie for Eeyore:

Cottleston, Cottleston, Cottleston Pie,
A fly can't bird, but a bird can fly.
Ask me a riddle and I reply:
"Cottleston, Cottleston, Cottleston Pie."

Cottleston, Cottleston, Cottleston Pie,
A fish can't whistle and neither can I.
Ask me a riddle and I reply:
"Cottleston, Cottleston, Cottleston Pie."

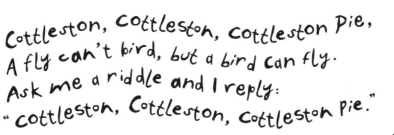

Cottleston, Cottleston, Cottleston Pie,
Why does a chicken, I don't know why.
Ask me a riddle and I reply:
"Cottleston, Cottleston, Cottleston Pie."

"That's right," said Eeyore. "Sing. Umty-tiddly, umpty-too. Enjoy yourself."

"I am," said Pooh. "But you seem so sad, Eeyore."

"Sad? Why should I be sad? It's my birthday. The happiest day of the year."

"Your birthday?" said Pooh, in great surprise.

"Of course it is. Can't you see? Look at all the presents I have had." He waved a foot from side to side.

Pooh looked – first to the right and then to the left.

"Presents?" said Pooh. "Where? I can't see them!"

"Neither can I," said Eeyore. "Joke," he explained. "Ha, ha!"

Pooh scratched his head being a little puzzled.

"But is it **really** your birthday?" he asked.

"It is."

"Oh! Well, **many happy returns** of the day, Eeyore."

"And many happy returns to you, Pooh Bear."

"But it isn't *my* birthday."

"No, it's mine."

"But you said 'Many happy returns' –"

"Well, why not? You don't want to be **miserable** on my birthday, do you?" said Eeyore. "It's bad enough being **miserable** myself, what with no presents and **no proper notice taken of me at all,** but if everybody else is going to be **miserable** too . . ."

This was **too much** for Pooh. "Stay there!" he called, as he hurried home; for he felt he must get Eeyore a **present** of some sort at once and he could always think of a proper one afterwards.

64

Outside his house, Pooh found Piglet jumping up and down trying to reach the knocker.

"What are you trying to do?" asked Pooh.

"I was trying to reach the knocker," said Piglet. "I just came round –"

"Let me do it for you," said Pooh, kindly.

So he reached up and knocked at the door.

"I have just seen Eeyore," he began, "poor Eeyore is very Gloomy because it's his birthday, and nobody has taken any notice of it, and what a long time whoever lives here is taking to answer this door."

"But Pooh," said Piglet, "it's your own house!"

"Oh!" said Pooh. "So it is. Well, let's go in."

So in they went.

The first thing Pooh did was to go to the cupboard to see if he had quite a small jar of honey left. And he had, so he took it down.

"I'm giving this to Eeyore," he explained, "as a **present**. What are you going to give?" "Couldn't I give it too?" said Piglet. "From **both** of us?" "No," said Pooh. "That would not be a **good plan**."

"All right, then, I'll give him a **balloon**. I've got one left from my party. I'll go and get it now, shall I?" said Piglet.

"That, Piglet, is a *very* good idea. It is just what Eeyore wants to **cheer** him up. Nobody can be **uncheered** with a balloon."

So off Piglet trotted, and in the other direction went Pooh, with his jar of honey.

Pooh hadn't gone more than half-way when a sort of
funny feeling began to creep all over him. It began
at the tip of his nose and trickled all through him and
out at the soles of his feet. It was just as if somebody
inside him were saying, 'Now then, Pooh, time for a
little something.'

So Pooh sat down to eat the honey.

As he took his **last lick**, he thought, "Now where was I going?" Then suddenly he remembered, **he had eaten Eeyore's birthday present!** Then he thought: "Well, it's a **very nice pot**, and if I washed it clean, and got somebody to write 'A Happy Birthday' on it, Eeyore could keep things in it, which might be **Useful**."

As Pooh was passing the Hundred Acre Wood, he went
to call on Owl, who lived there.

"Many happy returns of Eeyore's birthday," said Pooh.
"I'm giving Eeyore a **Useful Pot** to keep things in,
and I wanted to ask you –"
Owl looked at the pot. "You ought to write 'A Happy
Birthday' on it," he added.
"That was what I wanted to ask you," said Pooh.
"Because my spelling is **Wobbly** and the letters
get in the wrong places. Would you write
'A Happy Birthday' on it for me?"

"Can you read, Pooh?" Owl asked, a little anxiously. "There's a notice about **knocking** and **ringing** outside my door, which Christopher Robin wrote. Could you read it?"

"Christopher Robin **told** me what it said, and then I could," said Pooh.

"Well, I'll tell you what **this** says, and then you'll be able to," said Owl.

This is what Owl wrote:

HIPY PAPY BTHUTHDTH THUTHDA BTHUTHDY.

"I'm just saying 'A Happy Birthday'," said Owl, nervously.

"It's a nice **long one**," said Pooh, very much impressed by it.

"Well, actually, of course, I'm saying '**A very Happy Birthday** with love from Pooh.'"

While all this was happening, Piglet had gone back to his house to get Eeyore's balloon. He held it **tightly** against himself so it shouldn't **blow away**, and ran as fast as he could to get to Eeyore before Pooh so he would be the **first one** to give a present. And running along, thinking how pleased Eeyore would be, he tripped on a rabbit hole, and fell flat on his face.

Piglet wondered what had happened.
Had the Forest blown up?
Or had he and was he now alone on the moon
or somewhere?
Piglet got up.
He was still
in the
Forest!

"That's funny,"
he thought. "I
wonder what that bang was. And where's my
balloon? And what's that small piece of damp rag?"
It was the balloon!

"Oh, dear!" said Piglet. "Oh, dearie, dearie, dear!
I can't go back, and I haven't another balloon. Perhaps
Eeyore doesn't like balloons so very much."
So he trotted on, rather sadly now, and soon reached
Eeyore at the stream.

"Many happy returns of the day," said Piglet,
having now got closer.

Eeyore stopped looking at himself in the stream, and
turned to stare at Piglet.

"Just say that again," he said, as he balanced on three
legs, bringing his fourth leg up to his ear. He pushed
his ear forward with his hoof.

"Many happy returns of the day," said Piglet, again.

"My birthday?" said Eeyore.

"Yes, Eeyore, and I've brought you a present.
A balloon."

"Balloon?" said Eeyore. "One of those big coloured
things you blow up?"

"Yes, but I'm very sorry, Eeyore – I fell down."

"Dear, how unlucky! You didn't hurt yourself, Little Piglet?"

"No, but I – I – oh, Eeyore, I burst the balloon!"

There was a very long silence.

"My balloon?" said Eeyore at last.

Piglet nodded. "Yes, Eeyore," said Piglet, sniffing a little.
"Here it is. With – with many happy returns of the day."

And he gave Eeyore the small piece of damp rag.

"Is this it?" said Eeyore, a little surprised. "My present?"
Piglet nodded again.

"Thank you, Piglet," said Eeyore. "What colour was it
when it – when it was a balloon?"

"Red."

"My favourite colour," said Eeyore, thoughtfully.
"Well, well."

Piglet felt very miserable, and didn't know what to say.

Suddenly, there was Pooh.

"Many happy returns of the day," said Pooh.

"Thank you, Pooh, I'm having them," said Eeyore,
gloomily.

"I've brought you a little present," said Pooh, excitedly.

"It's a Useful Pot," said Pooh. "And it's got 'A Very
Happy Birthday with love from Pooh' written
on it. And it's for putting things in. There!"

When Eeyore saw the pot, he was quite excited.
"I believe my Balloon will go into that Pot!"
"Oh, no, Eeyore," said Pooh. "Balloons are much too
big to go into Pots."
"Not mine," said Eeyore proudly. "Look, Piglet!" And
as Piglet looked sadly round, Eeyore placed the balloon
carefully in the pot.
"So it does!" said Pooh. "It goes in!"
"So it does!" said Piglet. "And it comes out!"
"Doesn't it?" said Eeyore. "It goes in and
out like anything."

"I'm very glad," said Pooh, "that I thought of giving you a Useful Pot to put things in."

"I'm very glad," said Piglet, "that I thought of giving you Something to put in a Useful Pot."

But Eeyore wasn't listening. He was taking the balloon out, and putting it back again, as happy as could be.

Piglet Has
a Bath

Nobody seemed to know where they came from, but there they were in the Forest: Kanga and Baby Roo. Pooh asked Christopher Robin, "How did they come here?" Christopher Robin said, "In the Usual Way, if you know what I mean, Pooh."

And Pooh said, "Ah!" Then he went to call upon Piglet to see what he thought and at Piglet's house he found Rabbit, so they all talked about it.

"What I don't like about it is this," said Rabbit. "Here are we, all of us, and then suddenly, we wake up one morning, and what do we find? We find a Strange animal among us. An animal who carries her family about with her in her pocket!"

"The question is," said Piglet, "what are we to do about Kanga?"

"The best way," said Rabbit, "would be this. Hide Baby Roo and then when Kanga says, 'Where's Baby Roo?' we say, 'Aha!'"

"Aha!" said Pooh, practising.

"We say 'Aha!'" said Rabbit, "so Kanga knows that we know where Baby Roo is. 'Aha!' means 'We'll tell you where Roo is, if you promise to go away and never come back to the Forest.'"

"There's just one thing," said Piglet, fidgeting a bit.
"Christopher Robin said a Kanga was Generally
Regarded as One of the Fiercer Animals.
And it is well known that if One of the Fiercer Animals
is Deprived of Its Young, it becomes as fierce as
Two of the Fiercer Animals. In which case 'Aha!' is
perhaps a foolish thing to say!"

"Piglet," said Rabbit, "you haven't any pluck."

"It is hard to be brave," said Piglet, sniffing slightly,
"when you're only a Very Small Animal."

Rabbit, who had
begun to write
very busily,
looked up and
said: "It is
because you
are a Very Small
Animal that
you will be
Useful in the
adventure before us."

Piglet was so excited at the idea of being Useful that
he forgot to be frightened.

"What about me?" said Pooh sadly. "I suppose I shan't
be useful?"

"Never mind, Pooh," said Piglet comfortingly.

"Without Pooh," said Rabbit solemnly, "the adventure
would be impossible."

"Oh!" said Piglet, and tried not to look disappointed.

Pooh went into a corner of the room and said proudly
to himself, "Impossible without Me! That sort
of Bear."

"Now listen all of you," said Rabbit, when he had
finished writing, and Pooh and Piglet sat listening
very eagerly.

This was what Rabbit read out:

PLAN to CAPTURE BABY ROO

1 General Remarks. Kanga runs faster than any of Us, even Me.

2 More General Remarks. Kanga never takes her eye off Baby Roo, except when he's safely buttoned up in her pocket.

3 Therefore. If we are to capture Baby Roo, we must get a Long Start, because Kanga runs faster than any of Us, even Me. (See 1.)

4 A Thought. If Roo had jumped out of Kanga's pocket and Piglet had jumped in, Kanga wouldn't know the difference, because Piglet is a Very Small Animal.

5 Like Roo.

6 But Kanga would have to be looking the other way first, so as not to see Piglet jumping in.

7 See 2.

8 Another Thought. But if Pooh was talking to her very excitedly, she might look the other way for a moment.

9 And then I could run away with Roo.

10 Quickly.

11 And Kanga wouldn't discover the difference until Afterwards.

Rabbit

91

For a little while nobody said anything. And then Piglet said: "And – Afterwards? When Kanga does Discover the Difference?"

"Then we all say 'Aha!' Why, what's the trouble, Piglet?" said Rabbit.

"Nothing," said Piglet, "as long as we all three say it. I shouldn't care to say 'Aha!' by myself. It wouldn't sound nearly so well."

"Well, Pooh?" said Rabbit. "You see what *you* have to do?"

"No," said Pooh Bear. "Not yet," he said. "What do I do?"

"You just have to talk **very hard** to Kanga so as she doesn't notice anything."

"Oh! What about?"

"Anything you like."

"You mean like telling her a little bit of poetry or something?"

"That's it," said Rabbit. "Splendid. Now come along."

So they all went out to look for Kanga.

Kanga and Roo were in a sandy part of the Forest. Baby Roo was practising very small jumps in the sand, and falling down mouse-holes and climbing out of them. Kanga was saying, "Just one more jump, dear, and then we must go home."

And at that moment who should come stumping up the hill, but Pooh.

"Good afternoon, Kanga."

"Good afternoon, Pooh."

"We were just going home," said Kanga. "Good afternoon, Rabbit. Good afternoon, Piglet."

Rabbit and Piglet, who had come up from the other side of the hill, said "Good afternoon," and Roo asked them to look at him jumping, so they stayed and looked.

"Oh, Kanga," said Pooh, after Rabbit had winked at him twice, "I don't know if you are interested in Poetry at all?"

"Hardly at all," said Kanga.

"Oh!" said Pooh.

"Go on," said Rabbit, in a **loud whisper** behind
his paw.

"Talking of Poetry," said Pooh, "I made up a little piece
as I was coming along. It went like this. Er – now let
me see –"

"You must listen **very carefully**," said Rabbit to Kanga.

"So as not to miss any of it," said Piglet.

"Oh, yes," said Kanga, but she still looked at Baby Roo.

Pooh gave a little cough and began.

LINES WRITTEN BY
A BEAR OF VERY LITTLE BRAIN

On Monday, when the sun is hot
I wonder to myself a lot:
"Now is it true, or is it not,
"That what is which and which is what?"

On Tuesday, when it hails and snows,
The feeling on me grows and grows
That hardly anybody knows
If those are these or these are those.

On Wednesday, when the sky is blue,
And I have nothing else to do,
I sometimes wonder if it's true
That who is what and what is who.

On Thursday, when it starts to freeze
And hoar-frost twinkles on the trees,
How very readily one sees
That these are whose - but whose are these?

On Friday -

"Yes, it is, isn't it?" said Kanga, not waiting to hear what happened on Friday.

"Just one more jump, Roo, dear, and then we really must be going."

"Talking of Poetry," said Pooh quickly, "have you ever noticed that tree right over there?"

"No," said Kanga. "Jump in, Roo, dear, and we'll go home."

"You **ought** to look at that tree right over there," said Rabbit. "Shall I lift you in, Roo?" And he picked up Roo in his paws.

"I can see a bird in it from here," said Pooh. "Or is it a fish?"

"It isn't a fish, it's a bird," said Piglet.

"So it is," said Rabbit.

And then **at last** Kanga **did** turn her head to look. And the moment that her head was turned, Rabbit said in a **loud voice** "In you go, Roo!" and in jumped Piglet into Kanga's pocket, and off scampered Rabbit, with Roo in his paws, as fast as he could.

"Are you all right, Roo, dear?" said Kanga.

Piglet made a squeaky Roo-noise from the bottom
of Kanga's pocket.

"Rabbit had to go away," said Pooh. "I think he thought
of something he had to go and see about **suddenly**."

"And Piglet?"

"I think Piglet thought of something at the same
time. **Suddenly**."

"Well, we must be getting home," said Kanga.
"Goodbye, Pooh."

And in **three large jumps** she was gone.

99

Pooh looked after her as she went.

"I wish I could jump like that," he thought. "Some can and some can't. That's how it is."

But there were moments when Piglet wished that Kanga **couldn't**. Often, when he had had a long walk home through the Forest, he had wished that he were a bird; but now he thought jerkily to himself at the bottom of Kanga's pocket, "If this is flying I shall never really take to it."

And he was saying,

all the way to Kanga's house.

Of course as soon as Kanga unbuttoned her pocket, she saw what had happened. For a moment she was **frightened**, and then she knew she wasn't; for she felt sure that Christopher Robin would never let any harm happen to Roo. So she said to herself, "If they are having a joke with me, I will have a joke with them." "Now then, Roo, dear," she said, as she took Piglet out of her pocket. "Bedtime."

"Aha!" said Piglet, as well as he could after his **Terrifying Journey**. But it wasn't a very good "Aha!" and Kanga didn't seem to understand what it meant.

"Bath first," said Kanga
in a cheerful voice.
Piglet looked round
for the others.
But the others
weren't there!

Rabbit was playing with Baby Roo in his own house, and feeling more **fond** of him every minute,

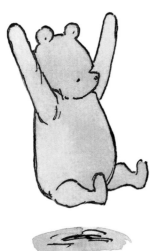

and Pooh, who had decided to be a Kanga, was **still** at the sandy place at the top of the Forest, practising jumps.

"I wonder," said Kanga, "if it would be a good idea to have a **cold bath** this evening. Would you like that, Roo, dear?"

Piglet had never been really fond of baths, so in as brave a voice as he could he said:

"Kanga, I am not Roo, I am Piglet!"

"Yes, dear, yes," said Kanga, soothingly. "And imitating Piglet's voice too! So clever of you," she went on, as she took a **large** bar of soap out of the cupboard.

"Can't you see?" shouted Piglet. "Haven't you got eyes? **Look at me!**"

"I am looking, Roo, dear," said Kanga **rather severely.** "And if you go on making faces like Piglet's, you will grow up to **look like Piglet** – and then think how sorry you will be. Now then, into the bath, and don't let me have to speak to you about it again."

Before he knew where he was, Piglet was in the bath, and Kanga was **scrubbing him firmly** with a **large** lathery flannel.

"Ow!" cried Piglet. "Let me out! **I'm Piglet!**"

"Don't open the mouth, dear, or the soap goes in," said Kanga. "There! What did I tell you?"

"You – you – you did it on purpose," spluttered Piglet, as soon as he could speak again.

"That's right, dear, don't say anything," said Kanga, and in another minute Piglet was out of the bath, and being rubbed dry with a towel.

PIGLET HAS A BATH

"Now," said Kanga, "there's your **medicine**, and then bed."

"W-w-what medicine?" said Piglet.

"To make you grow **big and strong**, dear. You don't want to grow up small and weak like Piglet, do you? Well, then!"

At that moment there was a knock at the door.

"Come in," said Kanga, and in came Christopher Robin.

"Christopher Robin!" cried Piglet. "Tell Kanga who I am! She keeps saying I'm Roo. I'm not Roo, am I?"
Christopher Robin looked at him very carefully, and shook his head.
"You can't be Roo," he said, "because I've just seen Roo playing in Rabbit's house."
"There you are!" said Piglet. "I told you so. I'm Piglet."
Christopher Robin shook his head again.
"Oh, you're not Piglet," he said. "I know Piglet well, and he's quite a different colour."
Piglet began to say that this was because he had just had a bath, and as he opened his mouth, Kanga slipped the medicine spoon in and patted him on the back.

"I knew it wasn't Piglet," said Kanga. "I wonder who
it can be?"

"Perhaps it's some relation of Pooh's," said
Christopher Robin.

Kanga agreed this was probably what it was, and said
that they would have to call it by some name.

"I shall call it Pootel," said Christopher Robin. "Henry
Pootel for short."

And just when this was decided, Henry Pootel wriggled
out of Kanga's arms and ran to the open door. Never had
Henry Pootel Piglet run so fast as he ran then. He didn't
stop running until he had got quite close to his house.
But when he was a hundred yards away, he stopped
running and

rolled

the rest

of the way home,

to get his own nice

comfortable

colour

again.

So Kanga and Roo stayed in the Forest. And every Tuesday Roo spent the day with his great friend Rabbit, and every Tuesday Kanga spent the day teaching her great friend Pooh to jump, and every Tuesday Piglet spent the day with his great friend Christopher Robin. So they were all happy again.